Whitney
the Whale
Fairy

To Antonia Bonewell,
a very special friend of the fairies!

Special thanks
to Narinder Dhami

No part of this work may be reproduced, stored in a retrieval system, or transmitted in any form or by any means, electronic, mechanical, photocopying, recording, or otherwise, without written permission of the publisher. For information regarding permission, write to Rainbow Magic Limited c/o HIT Entertainment, 830 South Greenville Avenue, Allen, TX 75002-3320.

ISBN 978-0-545-28876-7

12 11 10 9 8 7 6 5 4 3 2   11 12 13 14 15 16/0

Printed in the U.S.A.   40

First Scholastic printing, January 2011

Whitney
the Whale
Fairy

by Daisy Meadows

SCHOLASTIC INC.

New York   Toronto   London   Auckland
Sydney   Mexico City   New Delhi   Hong Kong

The Fairyland Palace

Fairyland Royal Aquarium

Kirsty's Gran's House

Lighthouse

The Park

Tide pool

Ocean Star Sailing Ship

Lea-On-Sea

Whales

With the magic conch shell at my side,
I'll rule the oceans far and wide!
But my foolish goblins have shattered the shell,
So now I cast my icy spell.

Seven shell fragments, be gone, I say,
To the human world to hide away,
Now the shell is gone, it's plain to see,
The oceans will never have harmony!

Contents

All Aboard the Ocean Star

"This is so much fun, Kirsty!" Rachel
Walker called to her best friend, Kirsty
Tate, as their ship, the *Ocean Star*, bobbed
across the waves. "Look, can you see
that school of fish?"

Kirsty peered over the ship's railing and
saw a group of tiny, silvery fish darting
through the sparkling turquoise water.
Some of the other girls and boys on the
boat trip rushed over to look, too.

"Leamouth looks so pretty in the sunshine, doesn't it?" Kirsty remarked, as they sailed across the bay. She and Rachel stood on the deck of the *Ocean Star*, enjoying the view of the seaside resort. From there they could see a long stretch of golden beach, and whitewashed cottages clustered around the harbor.

Kirsty and Rachel were spending their spring vacation in Leamouth with Kirsty's gran. Today, Gran had suggested that the girls take a special sailing trip just for kids. It was on an old-fashioned ship, run by Captain Andy and his crew.

Rachel and Kirsty were fascinated by the large wooden boat with its tall masts and billowing white sails.

"Ahoy there, sailors!" Captain Andy shouted, waving at the girls and boys on the deck below him. He stood behind the wooden ship's wheel, turning it back and forth to guide the boat through the water. "If you'd visited Leamouth hundreds of years ago, the harbor would have been full of large sailing ships just like the *Ocean Star*. There was one very famous boat called the *Mermaid*, but sadly it sank somewhere around this area a very long time ago."

"Do you know where the wreck is, Captain Andy?" asked Thomas, one of the boys on the trip.

Captain Andy shook his head. "We don't know exactly where the ship sank," he replied. "It had a beautiful carved and painted figure of a mermaid attached to its front. Legend says that the mermaid statue now watches over this area from wherever the wreck lies on the bed of the ocean."

"What a great story," Rachel said to Kirsty. "It sounds like magic!"

"We know all about *that*, don't we, Rachel?" Kirsty whispered, winking at her friend.

The two girls were right in the middle of another exciting, magical fairy adventure.

When they'd arrived in Leamouth, they'd received an invitation to visit the Fairyland Ocean Gala. There, they'd met their old friend Shannon the Ocean Fairy. Rachel and Kirsty had also been introduced to Shannon's helpers, the seven Ocean Fairies, and their magic ocean creatures, who lived in the Royal Aquarium.

Shannon explained to Rachel and Kirsty that the most important part of the Gala was when she played a song on the magic golden conch shell. The song ensured that there was peace and harmony in all the oceans for the next year.

Just as Shannon was preparing to play her song, Jack Frost and his goblins had barged in and disrupted the ceremony.

Jack Frost ordered the goblins to steal the golden conch shell, and they'd all rushed to grab it before the horrified fairies could stop them.

As the goblins fought over which one of them should carry the shell, they'd dropped it. With a crash, it had shattered into seven jagged pieces.

Jack Frost had been furious at the goblins' clumsiness! With a blast of icy

magic from his wand, he'd immediately
sent the shell pieces spinning through
the air to hide in
different places
throughout the
human world.
Both Jack Frost
and the fairies
knew that
without the magic
golden conch
shell, there would
be chaos and
confusion in the oceans.
Queen Titania had tried to limit the
power of Jack Frost's spell by using her
own magic to send the Ocean Fairies'
seven magic ocean creatures after the

shell pieces. They would guard them until they could be safely returned to Fairyland. Rachel and Kirsty were helping the Ocean Fairies in their quest, but they had to keep a careful lookout for Jack Frost's goblins. They were also searching for the missing fragments of shell.

"I wonder if we'll find another piece of the golden conch shell today," Kirsty murmured to Rachel as they sailed farther out to sea. "The shell's almost complete now. Only two more pieces left to find!"

"Don't forget—the queen always says that we have to wait for the

magic to come to us," Rachel reminded
her. "Let's just enjoy the boat trip and see
what happens!"

Suddenly Thomas gave a cry.

"What's *that*?" he shouted, pointing at
the foamy waves ahead of them. "I can
see something moving."

"Use your binoculars, sailors!"
Captain Andy called. All the passengers
had been given a set of binoculars when
they boarded the *Ocean Star*, and now
Rachel and Kirsty peered through theirs
eagerly. At first they couldn't see
much of anything, but then they both
noticed some flashes of movement on
the horizon.

"Wow!" Captain Andy exclaimed.
"The *Mermaid* has certainly brought

us good luck today. Look, everyone, there are whales!"

"Oh!" Rachel gasped with delight as she spotted a black-and-white whale surge up from beneath the waves and then splash down into the water again. "Oh, Kirsty, aren't they *beautiful*?"

"They're gorgeous!" Kirsty was breathless with excitement, her eyes glued to her binoculars. There were three whales surfacing now, blowing sparkling jets of water from their blowholes.

"They're orcas," Captain Andy explained as everyone watched the whales in delight. "Orcas belong to the dolphin family, and they often live in large family groups, called *pods*."

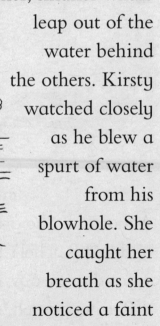

Just then, Kirsty noticed another, smaller whale leap out of the water behind the others. Kirsty watched closely as he blew a spurt of water from his blowhole. She caught her breath as she noticed a faint glimmer of silver sparkles all around the whale. She could hardly believe her eyes!

"Rachel, look!" Kirsty whispered, lowering her binoculars and turning to her friend. "That whale at the back is glowing with fairy magic. I think it's one of the magic ocean creatures from the Royal Aquarium. She grinned widely and grabbed Rachel's hand. "You know what that means, don't you?"

Rachel gasped, spotting the sparkles herself. Her eyes were big as she spun to

face Kirsty. "That must mean a piece of the golden conch shell is nearby!"

Whales at Play

Rachel's heart thumped with excitement. She stared through her binoculars and spotted the whale's glittering tail just before he dived below the waves again.

"You're right, Kirsty!" she said eagerly. "He must be Whitney the Whale Fairy's whale. I wonder if Whitney is somewhere around here, too."

"I'll steer the boat closer to the whales so we can all get a better look," Captain  Andy called, turning the ship's wheel. Everyone on board cheered. Rachel and Kirsty waited impatiently as the ship slowly changed course and began to move toward the whales. The girls couldn't help worrying that the whales might swim away before they reached them. The whales, however, seemed happy to frolic around in the ocean. They blew jets of water out their blowholes and spun in the ocean, flicking their tails back and forth. The whales seemed to be calling to one another every so often with strange, sweet sounds.

Suddenly, a loud burst of noise interrupted the peace of the ocean. Rachel and Kirsty spun around and saw a speedboat  zooming across the water toward the whales.

"Oh, no!" Rachel groaned, clapping her hands over her ears. "That noise is going to scare them away!"

Everyone on the *Ocean Star* watched anxiously as the speedboat headed straight at the whale pod. But suddenly, the driver of the boat slowed down and changed his course, beginning to head away from them.

"Thank goodness!" Kirsty sighed with relief. "The crew must have spotted the whales at the last minute."

To everyone's amazement, all the whales turned around and swam straight after the speedboat. Within a few

seconds, the whales were right behind
the boat. Then they moved up to swim
alongside it.

"Well, that's very
odd," Captain
Andy said,
looking
surprised.
"They
don't seem
bothered
by the
noise!"
The whales
splashed playfully
around the boat, sending
up sprays of water from their blowholes.
They didn't look scared at all.

"I think the speedboat is trying to get

away from them," Rachel pointed out as the boat began to weave from side to side.

"They're not having much luck though," Kirsty replied. "Look, the whales are *still* following them."

Captain Andy shook his head in astonishment. "I've never seen whales act this way before," he declared, looking very puzzled. "I just don't understand it."

Rachel and Kirsty glanced knowingly at each other.

"The whales are behaving strangely

because the golden conch shell is broken," Rachel whispered to Kirsty. "Nothing will be right in the oceans until the conch shell is whole again, so that Shannon can play it."

"Hello, girls!" called a tinkling, silvery voice all of a sudden. "Look over here!"

Kirsty grabbed Rachel's arm. "Rachel, did you hear that?" she asked.

Rachel nodded. "I think it came from down there!" she said, pointing over the side of the *Ocean Star*.

Everyone else was still watching the whales, so Rachel and Kirsty slipped away unnoticed and peered over the side.

"Look, Kirsty!" Rachel exclaimed. She pointed at an orange and white striped buoy floating on the water near the ship. Kirsty looked down and saw a tiny, glittering fairy perched on top of it.

"Hello, girls!" the fairy called again, waving at them. She had shiny black hair and she wore a floaty dress in deep shades of purple, yellow, and red, with matching yellow ballet slippers. "It's me, Whitney the Whale Fairy. I'm really worried about my whale, Fin! I know you've seen him playing with the other whales and chasing after that speedboat."

Rachel and Kirsty nodded.

"The problem is that Fin is following that boat farther and farther away from the part of the ocean where the shell piece is," Whitney went on anxiously. "We don't have much hope of finding the shell piece without Fin's help, so we need to stop him! Will you help me, girls?"

Seaweed Surprise

"Of course we'll help!" Rachel and Kirsty said together.

Whitney looked very relieved.

"Is it safe for me to come on board?" she asked.

Kirsty took a quick look over her shoulder. Everyone else was standing with their backs to the girls, still watching the whales.

"It looks safe, Whitney," Kirsty told her.

Whitney flew up, her wings dazzling in the bright sunlight, and landed on the ship's railing. "I'll turn you into fairies, girls," she whispered, lifting her wand. "Then we'll fly after Fin as fast as we can!"

Rachel and Kirsty saw a shower of magical sparkles spring from Whitney's wand and surround them.

Instantly, the girls felt themselves shrink down to fairy-size, complete with their own sets of glittering wings.

"Let's go!" Whitney cried, swooping off the side of the ship. "If we keep just above the waves, the movement of our wings will be masked by the sunlight glinting off the water. No one will be able to see us!"

Kirsty and Rachel followed Whitney, flying off the ship's railing and across the ocean. Below them, the white-tipped waves rolled and broke against the wooden sides of the ship.

"The *Ocean Star* looks even bigger now that we're fairy-size!" Rachel called to Kirsty as they headed toward Fin and the other whales.

The speedboat continued to circle and

weave its way through the water, but it
still hadn't managed to shake the whales.

"There's Fin!" Whitney
said. She pointed
out the small
whale with
the sparkly
tail that the
girls had
noticed earlier.

Fin swam happily along
behind the speedboat with another
whale.

"Can you call him, Whitney?" Kirsty
asked.

Whitney frowned. "I'm not sure he'll
hear me above the boat's motor," she
replied. "Let's go a little closer."

As Whitney and the girls flew toward the boat, Rachel noticed something strange about the crew. They all looked identical to one another, with very long noses and very large feet. And they were *green*. . . .

"Goblins!" Rachel exclaimed, pointing them out to Kirsty and Whitney.

"They must be looking for the shell piece, too," Kirsty said.

"The shell piece just might be closer than they think!" Whitney said in a dismayed voice. "Girls, look at Fin's tail. Can you see what I see?"

The girls stared down at the little whale's tail as it

splashed in and out of the water. They
could see a clump of green seaweed
caught on the end of it.

Then Rachel and Kirsty spotted a
gleam of magical golden light in the
middle of the seaweed.

"It's the missing shell piece!" Kirsty
gasped. "It's tangled up in the seaweed
on Fin's tail!"

"Which means that Fin *isn't* swimming
farther away from the shell piece at all,"
Whitney pointed out. "He's taking the
shell right to the goblins!"

"How can we stop him, Whitney?"
Rachel asked urgently.

Below them, the group of goblins
looked very panicky as the whales
continued to swim playfully around the
boat. They huddled together on the deck,

unsure what they should do.

"Go away, horrible fishy things!" the biggest goblin shouted. "We were only looking for the magic whale—we didn't want to be chased by *all* of you!"

"Why won't they stop following us?" the smallest goblin squeaked nervously.

Suddenly all the whales, including Fin, plunged under the water and out of sight. The goblins looked very relieved.

A few seconds later, the whales each resurfaced in a different place with a series of very loud splashes. Now, instead of being just behind the boat, Fin was swimming alongside of it.

One of the goblins gave a triumphant yell.

"I can see the missing piece of the golden conch shell!" he cried, his gaze fixed on Fin's tail.

"Fin, dive under the water again!"
Whitney yelled, flying over to him.
Rachel and Kirsty were right behind her.

But they were
too late. Fin
was so
surprised to
hear Whitney's
voice that he
stopped
swimming and
looked up. That gave the goblins just
enough time to lean over the side of the
boat and untangle the shell piece from
his tail.

"Got it!" the big goblin roared, waving
the shell in the air. "For once, we've
defeated those pesky fairies!"

The goblin who'd spotted the shell

scowled. "*I* saw it first!" he complained, "Give it to me!" He tried to grab the shell from the big goblin.

"Get off!" the big goblin howled. They each pulled at the piece of shell as though they were playing tug-of-war.

Suddenly, the gleaming golden shell slipped from their grasp. It sailed over the edge of the boat and landed in the ocean with a splash.

The two goblins turned to each other.

"Now look what you made me do!" they both said loudly, at exactly the same time.

"It's the fairies' fault!" one of the other goblins yelled. "They're always getting in the way and messing things up!"

Whitney turned to Rachel and Kirsty

as the goblins began arguing over who
was to blame.

"While the goblins are grumbling and
complaining, we can dive into the ocean
to find the shell piece!" she said. "Are
you ready, girls?"

Shipwreck!

Rachel and Kirsty nodded excitedly.

"Let's go!" Rachel cried.

Whitney waved her wand above the girls' heads and a mist of fairy dust appeared. When it settled, two shiny, translucent bubbles hovered in the air. The bubbles floated gently down. One settled over Rachel's head and the other over Kirsty's.

The girls weren't nervous at all, because this had happened to them several times before on their fairy adventures. They didn't even jump when the bubbles disappeared with a faint *pop*!

"Now you'll be able to breathe underwater," Whitney reminded them with a smile. "Down, down, down, we go!"

She dived into the waves headfirst, like a swimmer going off a diving board.

Rachel and Kirsty

followed. Below the water they saw Fin circling around waiting for them. He looked enormous to the girls now that they were fairy-size. He rushed over to greet them.

Fin looked dejected and made a sad songlike noise.

Whitney turned to the girls. "He didn't realize the shell piece was caught on his tail," she translated. "Don't worry." Whitney patted Fin's smooth, dark head. "It must be around here *somewhere*. Let's start looking for it right away."

Whitney, Rachel, Kirsty, and Fin swam slowly along just below the surface of the water, searching for the missing fragment of shell. Schools of pretty pink, blue, and yellow fish stared at  them curiously as they passed by. Suddenly, Kirsty gave a startled shout.

"Did you spot the shell?" Rachel asked eagerly.

"No, but look at that octopus!" Kirsty said, pointing. An octopus floated through the water upside down, waving its eight legs gracefully above its head.

"See those fish over there?" Kirsty

added. "Aren't they funny-looking?"

"Those are catfish," Whitney explained as the girls stared at the strange-looking fish with large eyes and whiskery mouths. As they watched, one of the catfish chased after a piece of driftwood floating in the water. He grabbed it in his mouth and took it back to the others.

Rachel and Kirsty couldn't believe what they were seeing!

"Catfish?" Rachel said with a grin. "They look more like *dogfish* to me!"

"Whitney, are they all acting strange because of the golden conch shell?" Kirsty asked.

Whitney nodded, her face serious. "This kind of chaos is going on in oceans all over the world," she said. "We *have* to find that missing piece before the goblins do!"

Suddenly Fin gave a squeak of warning and pointed a flipper up to the surface. There, spotlit by the bright sunshine above the ocean, were five dark shapes. They were swimming very quickly toward them.

"We need to hide, and quick!" Whitney declared. "Let's go deeper into the ocean, girls. Hurry!"

Whitney, Rachel, Kirsty, and Fin swam as fast as they could to the ocean floor. The water got darker the deeper

they went, but Rachel managed to spot
something.

"There's a big black shape at the very
bottom of the ocean just below us," she
told the others. "Maybe we can hide
underneath whatever it is."

They all headed toward it. As they got
closer, Kirsty turned to Rachel.

"I think it's a shipwreck!" she declared.

Kirsty was right. The enormous,
wooden hull of an old-fashioned sailing
ship like the *Ocean
Star* lay on the sandy
ocean floor. The masts
had broken in half and
the timbers were rotting
away. Brightly colored
fish darted in and out
of the portholes.

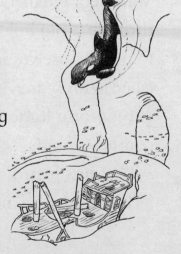

"The ship looks very old," Rachel observed as they swam closer.

Kirsty looked at her friend. "I wonder if this could be the shipwrecked *Mermaid* that Captain Andy told us about?"

Just then, a splashing sound behind them made everyone jump.

"The swimmers are catching up with us," Whitney said. "Hide!"

Fin swam around to the other side of the ship and hid behind a large rock. Whitney, Rachel, and Kirsty went through a big hole in the ship's deck and found themselves in a cabin that had filled with water. The cabin was empty except for a large wooden chest bobbing gently around.

The girls heard voices above them and Whitney put a finger to her lips. Quietly,

they turned to peek
out of the hole
they'd just swum
through.

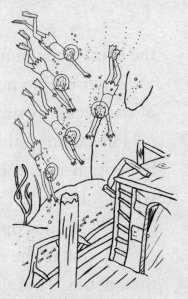

Five figures were
heading straight for
the shipwreck. As they
hovered above the
main deck, Rachel
could see that they had clear bubbles over
their heads and flippers on their feet.

"They're not humans," she whispered
urgently. "They're the goblins from the
speedboat!"

"We have to find the shell piece before
they do," Whitney said in a low voice.
"But be careful, girls!"

Silently, the three friends swam out of
the cabin and began to search the rest of

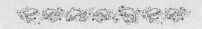

the ship. The goblins didn't notice. They were swimming across to the other end of the deck, toward the ship's wheel.

"The captain always stands here," the big goblin said importantly, grasping the wheel. "Because I'm bigger than all of you, *I'll* be the captain."

"Yes, you're the biggest," agreed one of the goblins, "but you're also the *silliest*! I'll be the captain. I'm the smartest!"

"Well, if you're so smart, what does *that* even do?" asked the smallest goblin, pointing to the wheel they were fighting over.

The second goblin looked a little sheepish. "I don't know," he confessed.

As the goblins bickered, Whitney and the girls split up so they could search the ship for the missing fragment of shell more quickly. Rachel began poking around the rotting timbers of one of the ship's masts, which lay on the deck.

As she peeked gently underneath a section of mast, the old wood crumbled at her touch and fell apart, sending debris up around her. Rachel was so surprised, she gasped loudly.

Immediately, all the goblins spun around.

"It's one of those pesky fairies!" the big goblin yelled. "We can make her show us where the shell piece is. Grab her!"

Treasure Trove

Even though they were on the other side
of the ship, Whitney and Kirsty heard
everything. They stared at each other in
horror.

"The goblins are going to capture
Rachel!" Whitney whispered. "We have
to stop them!"

Kirsty looked around desperately for
inspiration. Then she spotted the hole in

the deck where they'd hidden earlier.

"I have an idea," Kirsty announced. "Quick, Whitney, back to the cabin!"

They swam across to the gap in the wooden timbers and slipped down the hole into the waterlogged cabin again. The wooden chest still floated around the room, its lid half open. Kirsty went over to peer inside.

"Whatever was in here has rotted away," she told Whitney. "It's full of seashells and seaweed now. Fantastic!"

Whitney looked confused. "How is that going to help Rachel?" she asked.

"This looks like a treasure chest, right?" Kirsty replied with a grin. "With a little fairy magic, maybe we can make the seashells and seaweed look like treasure so we can distract the goblins!"

"What a great idea!" Whitney laughed. With a wave of her wand, she sent a shower of sparkles raining down on the wooden chest. Kirsty grinned as the shells and seaweed were transformed into shining golden crowns and long necklaces of glittering emeralds, rubies, sapphires, and diamonds.

"Let's hope this works," Whitney whispered to Kirsty as they swam back up to the deck. "I don't know how long my magic will last."

Outside, Rachel was darting around, trying desperately to escape from the goblin's clutches.

"Hey, Rachel!" Kirsty called loudly. "Forget about that silly shell piece. We found something even better in this cabin—a chest full of treasure!"

All the goblins whirled around.

"TREASURE!" they roared excitedly. "Hooray!"

Losing all interest in Rachel, the goblins swam speedily across the deck and down into the cabin.

"Are you all right, Rachel?" Whitney asked as she hurried to join her. Rachel

nodded gratefully. Meanwhile, Kirsty
was peeking through the hole in the deck
at the goblins in the cabin below.

"The goblins are draping themselves
in the necklaces and wearing the crowns
on their heads!" Kirsty laughed.

"Well, the goblins are out of the way
for the moment," Whitney said. "But

we've looked everywhere and we *still* haven't found the shell."

"Maybe Fin can help," Rachel suggested.

"Fin!" Whitney called. "Where are you?"

Fin gave a low whale song in reply. He swam out from behind the rock. Fin hovered near the prow of the shipwreck, which was covered in large clumps of seaweed. Whitney and the girls swam over to him.

Fin gestured at the ship's prow with his flipper.

"There's something hidden under the seaweed," Whitney said excitedly.

Rachel and Kirsty helped Whitney pull the feathery green fronds aside. Underneath, they found a carved wooden figure of a mermaid. She was beautiful, with long flowing hair and a fish's tail.

"So this shipwreck is the *Mermaid* after all!" Kirsty exclaimed.

"She's lovely." Rachel sighed, gazing at the mermaid's pretty, serene face.

Kirsty nodded, then gave a cry of surprise. "Look at the mermaid's hair!" she said.

Whitney, Rachel, and Fin stared closely. Nestled in the mermaid's long flowing locks like a golden comb, was the missing shell piece! The girls couldn't believe it!

Just as Rachel reached out her hand to grab it, the goblins swam up onto the deck. They wore strands of seaweed around their necks and large shells on their heads. They looked *very* silly and *very* angry.

"It looks like my magic has worn off!"
Whitney whispered.

"Look, there's the shell piece!" the big
goblin yelled, pulling the seaweed off his
neck. "Let's grab it!"

Goblin Fountains!

"Quick, Fin!" Whitney said, as the goblins began to swim toward them. "We need your help!"

Fin nodded. He opened his mouth and a beautiful whale song poured out, echoing throughout the depths of the ocean. Rachel and Kirsty had never heard anything quite so amazing.

Suddenly, an answering call came from deep in the ocean. A few moments later, the girls gasped as the other whales came diving down through the water toward them at very high speed. The goblins' eyes almost popped out of their heads when they saw the enormous whales heading in their direction.

"Let's get out of here!" they yelled. Forgetting all about the shell, they turned and began to swim away as fast as they could.

But the whales were much better swimmers. Five of them swam up behind the goblins. Each of the whales scooped up one of the goblins gently with their noses, tipping them onto their backs. All of the goblins shrieked with fear as the whales headed back up to the surface of the ocean.

"Let us go, you horrible things!" the smallest goblin yelled as he was carried off.

Immediately, Rachel grabbed the shell piece from the mermaid's hair.

"Thank you," she whispered to the carved figure.

"Grab onto Fin's tail, girls, and we'll follow the other whales!" Whitney told them.

The girls did as she said. Fin went

rushing back toward the surface of the ocean, pulling Whitney, Kirsty, and Rachel easily behind him. As they broke through the waves into the sunlight again, they all burst out laughing at the scene in front of them.

The whales that had picked up the goblins were shooting tall fountains from their blowholes. The goblins were bouncing around on top of the huge jets of water, unable to escape. The goblins looked extremely upset.

"Let me go!" one of them shouted, "I don't want to be a goblin fountain!"

Other whales swam around them, performing graceful flips, turns, and rolls in the water. It was a magical sight.

Whitney turned to Rachel and Kirsty. "I don't think the goblins are going to bother us again for a little while!" she said. "Time to take you back to the *Ocean Star*, girls." Whitney waved her wand.

Immediately, Fin shrank down to his fairy-size. Whitney tucked the whale firmly under her arm. Then, with another flick of her wrist, she

whisked them all back to the deck of the *Ocean Star*.

Luckily, Captain Andy and everyone else on board was still at the other end of the deck, and didn't notice their arrival. Whitney quickly used her magical fairy dust to make Rachel and Kirsty their normal size again.

"That was a fantastic fairy adventure!" Kirsty sighed happily. "I'm so glad we found the shell piece."

"Now there's only one piece left to find before the magic golden conch shell is whole again," Rachel added.

"Thank you so much, girls," Whitney said. "Fin and I couldn't have done it without you. Now we have to take the shell back to Fairyland. Shannon and the other Ocean Fairies are going to be thrilled!"

Rachel and Kirsty gave Fin a good-bye pat. They waved as Whitney and her whale disappeared in a flurry of glittering sparkles.

"Rachel! Kirsty!" Thomas came running over to the girls, looking very excited. "The whales are back! They disappeared for a little while, but now they're here again. Aren't we lucky to see them?"

"Yes," Kirsty replied, exchanging a secret smile with Rachel. "We're *very* lucky!"

THE OCEAN FAIRIES

Whitney the Whale Fairy has found her
piece of the golden conch shell!
Now Rachel and Kirsty
must help . . .

Courtney
the Clownfish Fairy!

Join their next underwater adventure
in this special sneak peek. . . .

Where's Courtney?

"I can't believe that we're going home tomorrow," Rachel Walker said, gazing out to sea. "This has been such a terrific vacation!"

"I know," her best friend, Kirsty Tate, agreed. "I'll never forget it."

The two girls leaned against the

railing at the end of Leamouth Pier. It was a warm, clear day and the sun cast dancing sparkles on the water below. Bouncy music boomed out from the carnival behind them.

Rachel sighed. "I'm a little worried. We still haven't found the last piece of the conch shell and time's running out."

"We can't let our vacation end without finding it," Kirsty replied. "I really hope we meet Courtney the Clownfish Fairy soon!"

The girls gazed at the carnival rides, hoping they might see the little fairy. There was a giant spiral slide, a bouncy castle, a spinning octopus ride, and lots of game booths. "Is that a sparkle of fairy dust near the slide?" Kirsty asked, pointing.

Rachel shaded her eyes to see. "No,"

she replied sadly. "It's just the flash from a camera." She linked her arm with Kirsty's. "It's no use for us to search for Courtney," she continued. "Remember what Queen Titania always says? We don't need to look for fairy magic. It will find its way to us."

Kirsty nodded. "You're right," she said. "Come on, let's go to the carnival. Look, there's a clown over there."

The girls wandered closer to the clown. He was wearing a red-and-white polka-dotted jumpsuit, a little black hat with a yellow flower on top, huge floppy shoes, and full clown makeup. He was busy bending balloons into shapes. The girls watched as he turned a red balloon into a dog for a little girl, and a blue balloon into a sword for a boy.

The clown saw them watching and waved. "Hello!" he called. "Let me make something for you."

He pulled out a long orange balloon and twisted it into the shape of a fish. "Here you go! Don't let him swim away!"

"Thank you," Kirsty said, taking the fish balloon. As the clown walked away, Kirsty's heart skipped excitedly.

A magical glimmer was coming from inside the balloon. As she looked closer, she realized it was Courtney the Clownfish Fairy!

RAINBOW magic™

There's Magic in Every Series!

The Rainbow Fairies

The Weather Fairies

The Jewel Fairies

The Pet Fairies

The Fun Day Fairies

The Petal Fairies

The Dance Fairies

The Music Fairies

The Sports Fairies

The Party Fairies

Read them all!

RAINBOW magic

These activities are magical!
Play dress-up, send friendship notes,
and much more!

■ SCHOLASTIC

www.scholastic.com
www.rainbowmagiconline.com

HIT entertainment

RMACTIV